For Mom & Dad

Copyright © 2015 by Elise Parsley • Cover art © 2015 by Elise Parsley • Cover design by Patti Ann Harris • Cover © 2015 Hachette Book Group, Inc. • All rights reserved. In accordance with the U.S. Copyright Act of 1976, the scanning, uploading, and electronic sharing of any part of this book without the permission of the publisher is unlawful piracy and theft of the author's intellectual property. If you would like to use material from the book (other than for review purposes), prior written permission must be obtained by contacting the publisher at permissions@hbgusa.com. Thank you for your support of the author's rights.

Little, Brown and Company • Hachette Book Group • 1290 Avenue of the Americas, New York, NY 10104 • Visit us at lb-kids.com • Little, Brown and Company is a division of Hachette Book Group, Inc. • The Little, Brown name and logo are trademarks of Hachette Book Group, Inc. • The publisher is not responsible for websites (or their content) that are not owned by the publisher. • First Edition: July 2015

Library of Congress Cataloging-in-Publication Data • Parsley, Elise, author, illustrator. • If you ever want to bring an alligator to school, don't! / written and illustrated by Elise Parsley.—First edition. • pages cm • Summary: A child provides insights, based on personal experience, into everything that can go wrong if one brings an alligator to school for show-and-tell. • ISBN 978-0-316-37657-0 (hardcover)— ISBN 978-0-316-37658-7 (ebook) [1. Alligators—Fiction. 2. Schools—Fiction. 3. Show-and-tell presentations—Fiction. 4. Humorous stories. • I. Title. • PZ7.P2495If 2015 • E]—dc23 • 2014015917 • 10 9 8 7 6 5 4 3 • APS • PRINTED IN CHINA

# If You Ever Want to Bring an Alligator to School, DON'T!

written and illustrated by

**Elise Parsley**

L B

Little, Brown and Company
New York Boston

If your teacher tells you
to bring something
from nature for
show-and-tell, she means
a hollow stick,
or a bird's nest,
or some sparkly rocks.

She does **not** want you to bring an alligator.

If you bring an alligator anyway, she'll tell you that

alligators are trouble!

You'll tell her that it's okay and that you know all about alligators. This alligator will be quiet and good, and he won't eat anyone— cross your heart.

This is because the alligator
will be showing you funny pictures.

Your teacher will write your name
on the board,

and now you'll have to stand last in line for lunch.
You'll take away the crayons and tell the
alligator to be quiet and wait for show-and-tell.

Then during art,

This is because the alligator
will be showing you origami.

Your teacher will draw a check
by your name,

Magnolia✓

and now you'll have to stay in from recess.
You'll take away the paper and
order the alligator
to be good
and wait for show-and-tell.

During math,

you'll notice
the alligator is hungry.

You'll give the alligator
three pieces
of your favorite gum

and your teacher will notice.

She'll draw two more checks by your name,

Magnolia ✓✓✓

and an underline.

Magnolia ✓✓✓

Now you'll have to go to the principal's office after school.

During lunch, you won't even
get to eat your egg-and-cheese
sandwich, because Somebody
will gobble up everything but
the crusts.

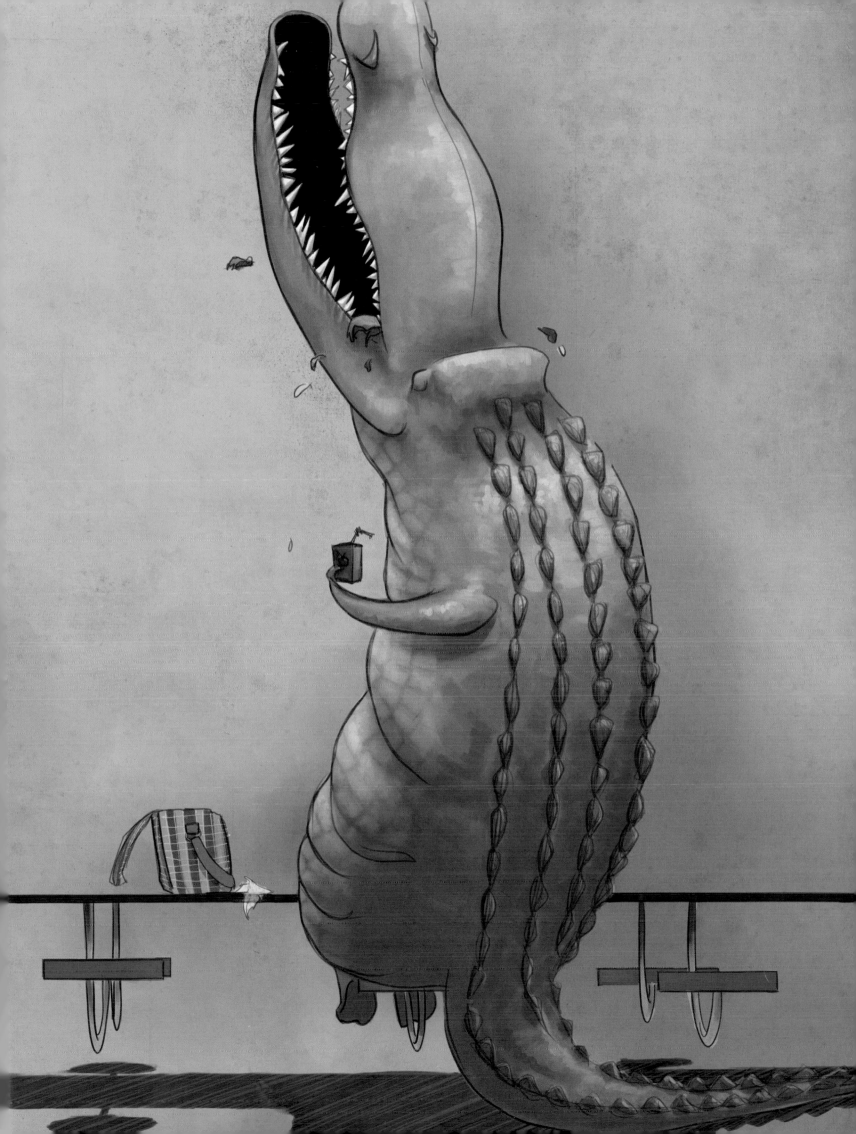

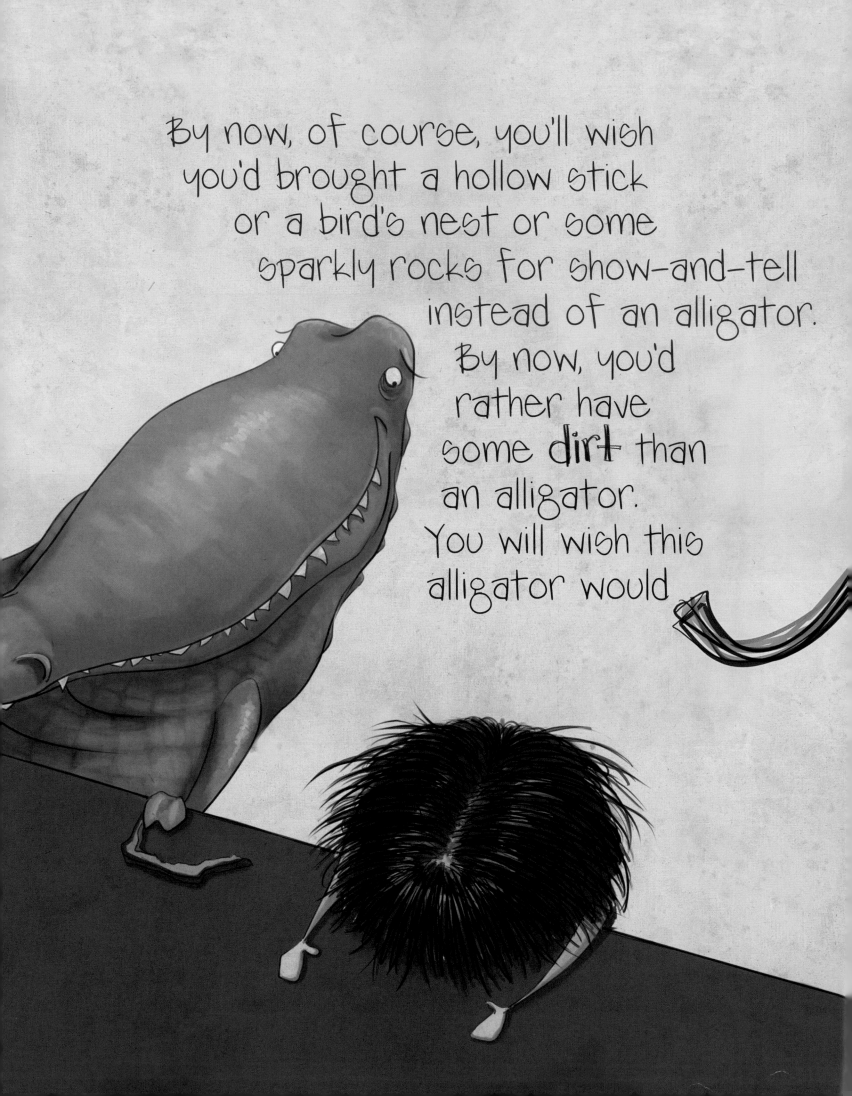

By now, of course, you'll wish
you'd brought a hollow stick
or a bird's nest or some
sparkly rocks for show-and-tell
instead of an alligator.
By now, you'd
rather have
some dirt than
an alligator.
You will wish this
alligator would

just go home!

Well, here's what I would do
if I were you:

First, at show-and-tell,
you'll sit quietly and learn
about hollow sticks

and birds' nests

and sparkly rocks.

Then...

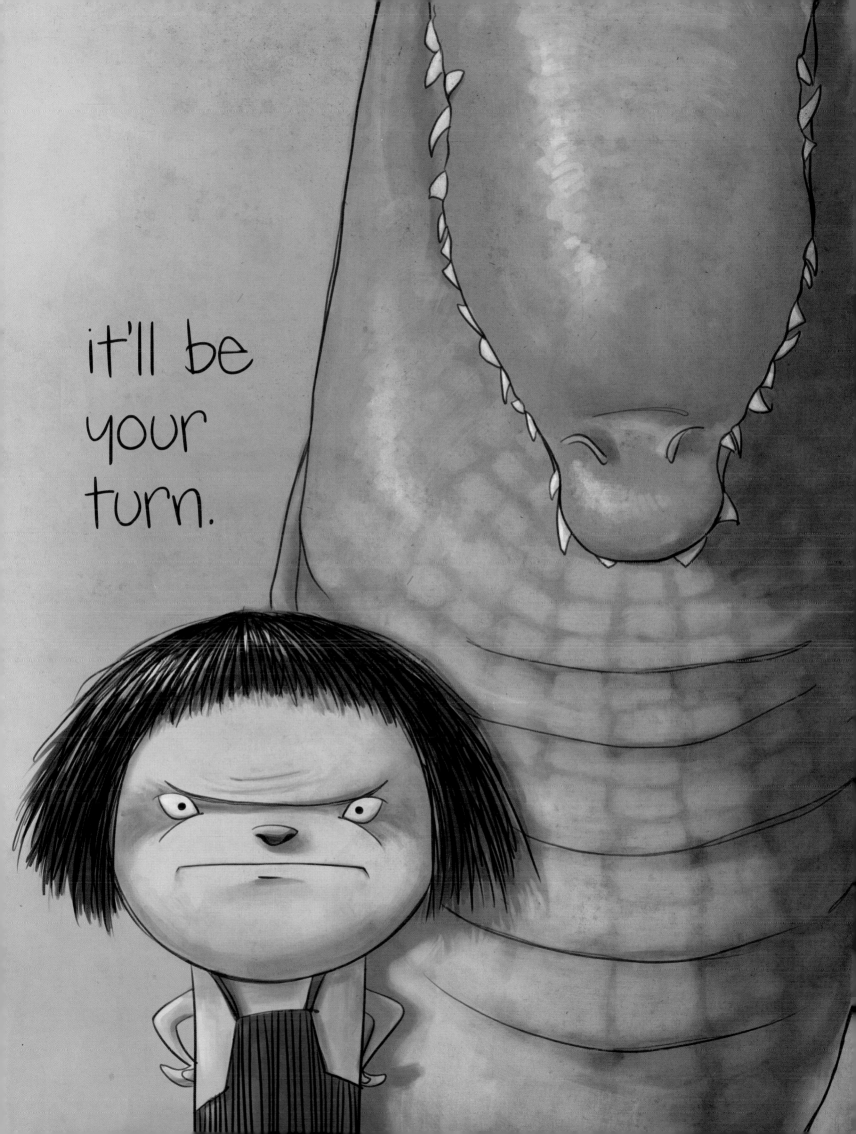

and how alligators
are super tough.
It's a fact.
They're strong and
they're tough and
they aren't scared
of anything
except other
alligators...

and humans.

Your teacher will be impressed.
You might not even have to go
to the principal's office
for all the mischief that day.

But then again...

you might have to.

PRINC